When Nana Dances

For Heidi E. Y. Stemple, without whom I wouldn't have
Maddison Stemple-Piatt to play and write with— JY

To Nana, the best dance partner, and Mama, who drove me
to every ballet class and made every costume— MSP

In honor of my children's Nana, Lily Garcia,
and Grandma, Harriet Burris— PB

Books for Kids From the
American Psychological Association

Text copyright © 2021 by Jane Yolen and Maddison Stemple-Piatt. Illustrations copyright © 2021 by
Priscilla Burris. Published in 2021 by Magination Press, an imprint of the American Psychological
Association.

Magination Press is a registered trademark of the American Psychological Association. Order books at
maginationpress.org, or call 1-800-374-2721.

Book design by Rachel Ross
Printed by Sonic Media Solutions, Inc., Medford, NY

Library of Congress Cataloging-in-Publication Data
Names: Yolen, Jane, author. | Stemple-Piatt, Maddison, author. | Burris, Priscilla, illustrator.
Title: When Nana dances/Jane Yolen, Maddison Stemple-Piatt; [illustrated by] Priscilla Burris.
Description: Washington, DC: Magination Press, [2021] | Summary: Nana shimmies, bops, taps, and twirls
her way to a shindig with her grandchildren, who love dancing with their grandmother.
Identifiers: LCCN 2020042595 (print) | LCCN 2020042596 (ebook) | ISBN 9781433836848 (hardcover) | ISBN
9781433836855 (ebook)
Subjects: CYAC: Grandmothers—Fiction. | Dance—Fiction.
Classification: LCC PZ8.3.Y76 Wfn 2021 (print) | LCC PZ8.3.Y76 (ebook) | DDC [E]—dc23
LC record available at https://lccn.loc.gov/2020042595
LC ebook record available at https://lccn.loc.gov/2020042596

Manufactured in the United States of America
10 9 8 7 6 5 4 3 2 1

When Nana Dances

by Jane Yolen and Maddison Stemple-Piatt

illustrated by Priscilla Burris

Magination Press · Washington, DC · American Psychological Association

When Nana dances,
on the wooden floor

why, she
shakes-a-shake
I've never seen before.

She twirls
and whirls
around the room,

dancing with umbrellas,
a rake, or a broom.

Oh—she's a sight to see.

When Nana dances—
then whoa—Nana dances.
Oh, how Nana dances with me.

She says that once
she danced on toe,
in flowing tutus
swinging low.

She says that once—

brush, scuff, and slap—
she crossed the stage

with a tap-tap-tap.

She can *shimmy*,

she can *mambo*,

and do the *bunny hop.*

And, she says,
she can still make
traffic **stop**.

That she's a wonder,

It's easy to see.

When Nana dances—
then wow—Nana dances.
Oh, how Nana dances with me.

But of all her dances,
the finest by far
is when she dances
to Papa's guitar. . .

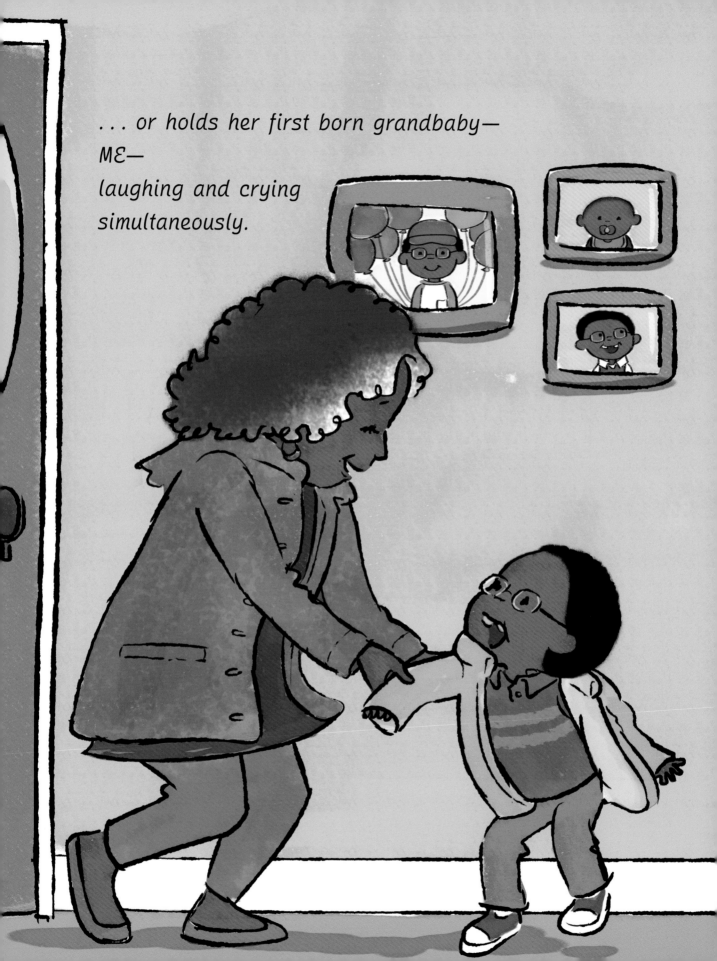

... or holds her first born grandbaby—
ME—
laughing and crying
simultaneously.

Now she dances when we walk.

She dances when we stroll.

She dances with
her blue ribbons and
big silver bowl.

She does *east coast swing,*

and a
buck
and
wing

and her **salsa** makes
the rafters sing.

We watch her steps on the TV.

But I think that we can all agree
that the best is when she dances,

most fun is when she dances,

I *love* when Nana dances
with MƐ!

Jane Yolen is the author of over 400 books for children and adults. Her books, stories, and poems have won many awards including the Caldecott Medal, two Nebula Awards, two Christopher Medals, three Golden Kite Awards, and the Jewish Book Award. She lives in Hatfield, MA.

Visit janeyolen.com, @Jane.Yolen on Facebook, @JaneYolen on Twitter, and @JYolen on Instagram.

Maddison Stemple-Piatt is Jane's first grandchild. Following in her Nana's footsteps, she trained in ballet from a young age.She has earned her bachelor's in Psychology with minors in Spanish and Dance, her master's in Criminology and Criminal Justice, and is currently a Juris Doctor candidate. She lives in St. Petersburg, FL.

Priscilla Burris is an author-illustrator and a member of the board of advisors for the Society of Children's Book Writers and Illustrators. Priscilla is represented by the CAT Agency, Inc. She lives in Southern California.

Visit priscillaburris.com and @PriscillaDesign on Twitter and Instagram.

Magination Press is the children's book imprint of the American Psychological Association. APA works to advance psychology as a science and profession and as a means of promoting health and human welfare. Magination Press books reach young readers and their parents and caregivers to make navigating life's challenges a little easier. It's the combined power of psychology and literature that makes a Magination Press book special.

Visit maginationpress.org and @MaginationPress on Facebook, Twitter, Instagram, and Pinterest.